15.00 7/1/17

WITHDRAWN

¿Qué tiempo hace? / What's the Weather Like?

Hace Sol
It's Sunny

Celeste Bishop

traducido por / translated by
Charlotte Bockman

ilustrado por / illustrated by
Maria José Da Luz

PowerKiDS press.

New York

Published in 2017 by The Rosen Publishing Group, Inc.
29 East 21st Street, New York, NY 10010

First Edition

Managing Editor: Nathalie Beullens-Maoui
Editor: Caitie McAneney
Book Design: Michael Flynn
Spanish Translator: Charlotte Bockman
Illustrator: Maria José Da Luz

Cataloging-in-Publication Data

Names: Bishop, Celeste.
Title: It's sunny = Hace sol / Celeste Bishop.
Description: New York : Powerkids Press, 2016. | Series: What's the weather like? = ¿Qué tiempo hace? | In English and Spanish. | Includes index.
Identifiers: ISBN 9781499423303 (library bound)
Subjects: LCSH: Sunshine–Juvenile literature. | Weather–Juvenile literature. | Sun–Juvenile literature.
Classification: LCC QC911.2 B57 2016 | DDC 551.5'271–dc23

Manufactured in the United States of America

CPSIA Compliance Information: Batch #BS16PK: For Further Information contact Rosen Publishing, New York, New York at 1-800-237-9932

Contenido

Contents

Está cálido y resplandeciente fuera. ¡Hace sol!

It's warm and bright outside. It's sunny!

El sol sale por la mañana.

The sun comes up in the morning.

Es un círculo grande en el cielo.

It's a big circle in the sky.

7

Cuando hace sol juego fuera.

I play outside when it's sunny.

¡Mis amigos también juegan fuera!

My friends play outside, too!

9

Nos gusta jugar al fútbol.

We like playing soccer.

¡Anoto un gol!

I score a goal!

¡El sol nos da calor!

The sun makes us hot!

Tomamos helado para refrescarnos.

We eat ice cream to cool off.

Los días muy soleados mi familia va a la playa.

On really sunny days, my family goes to the beach.

Nos sirve para refrescarnos.

It helps us cool off.

Mi mamá dice que mucho sol puede dañar mi piel.

My mom says too much sun can hurt my skin.

Me pongo protector solar.

I wear sunscreen.

También me pongo gafas
para proteger mis ojos.

I also wear sunglasses in the sun.
They keep my eyes safe.

19

El sol ayuda a las personas y a las plantas.

The sun helps people and plants.

20

Las plantas usan el sol para producir alimento.

Plants use the sun to make food.

El sol se acuesta en la noche.
¡Mañana lo volveremos a ver!

The sun goes to bed at night.
We'll see it again tomorrow!

23

Palabras que debes aprender
Words to Know

(el) helado
ice cream

(las) gafas
sunglasses

(el) protector solar
sunscreen

Índice / Index

24